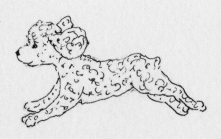

Published by Octobre Press

736 22nd Place, Vero Beach, Florida 32960

Illustrations by Virginia Best

Editorial Development by Laura Ross

Art Editing by Cynthia Bardes

Assistant Art Editing by David and Ralph

PRINTED IN THE UNITED STATES

This book was typeset in Berkeley.

ISBN 978-0-692-61301-6

Pansy in New York

The Mystery of the Missing Monkey

written by Cynthia Bardes

illustrations by Virginia Best

Other titles in this series

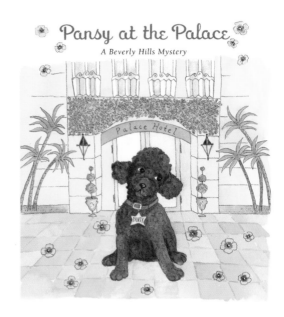

Pansy toy dog

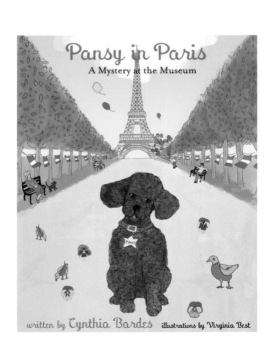

www.PansythePoodle.com

Please visit the website for more information

for Avery, Aubrey, Cindy, and David

My name is Pansy.
My best friend Avery and I
have solved mysteries
all over the world.
As a reward for our hard work,
Mama and Daddy
brought us to New York City!

Avery wanted to see the dinosaurs
in the Natural History Museum, so that was our first stop.

Afterwards, Avery said, "Let's walk down Fifth Avenue."
We passed lots of pretty shops filled with toys, jewelry, and clothes,
then stopped in front of a very fancy store.

"Oooh, the windows look like fairy tales," said Avery.

I stopped at a hot dog cart.
"Woof, woof!" I said. *I'm hungry.*

I wanted to visit the animals
at the Central Park Zoo more than anything. We rode there
in a carriage pulled by a horse with a feather on his head.

On the way, we passed a strange man in a cape and top hat carrying a big purple bag.
He was buying peanuts.

We said hello to the seals and penguins. We pretended to be sea lions and made funny noises. "Arrr, arrr, aaaarrrhhh." Then we followed the signs leading to Morris the Talking Monkey.

MONKEY WORLD →

VISIT MORRIS the TALKING MONKEY

When we got to the snow monkeys,
the zookeeper was crying and Mama and Papa
monkey were crying, too. Morris the Talking
Monkey was gone!
A policeman showed up to help.

Avery said, "Officer, this is Pansy the famous
poodle detective. She has already solved
three mysteries and maybe she can help find Morris!"

"Here is a picture of Morris," the zookeeper said. "He likes peanuts and pink marshmallows and he LOVES bananas!"

"Those are good clues," said Avery.

"Woof, woof," I said. *Let's go find Morris!*

"Good luck," said the policeman.

As we passed the tropical birds,
I noticed something. A line of peanut shells!
"Where there are peanut shells, there might be a monkey. . . ." Avery whispered.
"Yip, yip!" I followed the peanut shells all the way to the front gate of the zoo
and kept going!

Marshmallow Heaven
FLAVORS · COLORS · SHAPES

MARSHMALLOW
☆ ANIMALS ☆

MARSHMALLOW
HEARTS & FLOWERS

CUSTOM
MARSHMALLOW
BOUQUETS

ON SALE
TODAY!
ALL
PINK
MARSHMALLOWS

The peanut shells led us straight to a shop
called Marshmallow Heaven.

"Look at my store!" cried the shopkeeper. "Someone
ate all of my pink marshmallows and left a big sticky mess!"

I saw a trail of funny pink footprints.

"Hmmm," said Avery.

"Shlurp, shlurp," I said, licking sweet pink goo off my nose.

We followed the pink footprints to a fruit store.
A man stood holding an empty basket
and there were banana peels all over the ground.

"A monkey took all of my bananas! I couldn't catch him," he said.
"Please find him—but be careful not to slip!"

We followed the banana peels to a giant building
with wide steps and big columns. The sign said Metropolitan Museum of Art.

"Morris could be close by!" said Avery.

"Yip, yip!" *Let's check inside.*

I barked and started to run. Avery raced after me.

I stopped in my tracks. *Sniff, sniff, sniff.*
I could smell peanuts and bananas, and . . .
something else.

Could it be a monkey?

My nose led us to a room filled with mummies,
masks, and mysterious objects.

"AWOOOO," we heard and I jumped straight up in the air!

Avery looked around and shouted,
"Morris! Is that you?"

"Yes, it's me," said the monkey as he landed on a big gold throne.

"How did you get here?" asked Avery.

"A man came to visit Monkey World. He was a magician and asked me to join his show. That sounded like fun! I was curious to see outside the zoo."

"So I went with him. He gave me a bag of peanuts."

"Pansy found you by following the peanut trail you made," said Avery.

"I got homesick and ran away," said Morris. "I saw a marshmallow store. I love pink marshmallows so I ate and ate! Then I saw a fruit stand with bananas. Now I have a tummy ache and I am lost."

"Let's get you home to your Mama and Papa," said Avery. "On the way, you can stop and apologize for the mess you made."

Aarf, aarf, I added, and licked Morris's monkey face.

"This is Morris the Talking Monkey," Avery told the shopkeepers. "We are taking him back to the zoo, but first he wanted to see you."

"I am very sorry I messed up your stores," said Morris. "The marshmallows and bananas looked so delicious. I was lost and hungry."

"Thank you for coming back to apologize, Morris," said the marshmallow lady. "I wish you had asked us for help."

"If you had told us you were lost and hungry, we would have fed you and helped you get home," said the fruit man. "Never be afraid to ask for help."

When we got back to the zoo, Morris's Mama and Papa wrapped their fuzzy arms around him in a big hug and swept him up into their favorite tree.

The zookeeper cheered and so did all the other monkeys.

Suddenly, Morris pointed and shouted, "That's Max the Magician!"

"Thank goodness you got back safely, Morris!" said Max. "I was wrong to take you with me. When you ran away, I was so worried! I tried to find you so I could bring you home."

The zookeeper grabbed Max by the arm. "Why did you take Morris?" he shouted.

"I wanted a talking monkey for my magic show," replied Max. "Morris said he wanted to come with me."

"Taking Morris from the zoo was wrong," said the police officer.

"Please don't punish Max!" said Morris. "I wanted to be in a
show and see the world! I'm sorry I left without asking Mama and Papa."

"I have an idea," said Avery. "Morris, why don't you and Max do a magic
show here? We can invite all the animals."

"Yip, yip, whoohoo!" I said, jumping up and down.

"Splendid!" said the zookeeper.

"Wonderful!" said the police officer. "Thank you for helping us find Morris. How can we reward you?"

"We want to see New York City!" said Avery.

"You've got it!" the officer replied with a big smile. "I'll pick you up first thing tomorrow morning for a special tour."

"Yip, yip!" I sang and danced.

The next morning, we sped around the Statue of Liberty in a special boat. The policeman let us turn on the siren. *Wooooo, woooo, wooooo!*

That night, we went to see a play on Broadway called *Poodleful!*
It is a story about a little dog just like me. I sang along—"hoooo, hoooo"—until Avery said,
"Shhhhh."

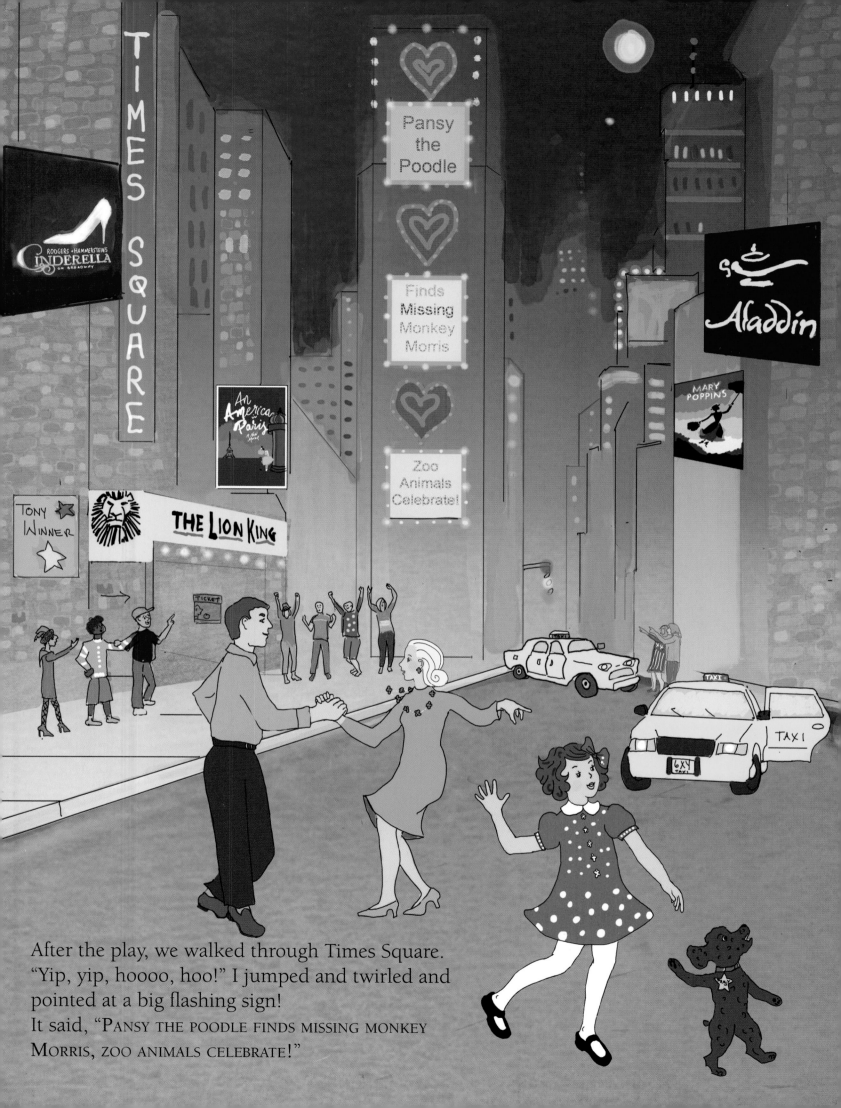

After the play, we walked through Times Square.
"Yip, yip, hoooo, hoo!" I jumped and twirled and
pointed at a big flashing sign!
It said, "PANSY THE POODLE FINDS MISSING MONKEY
MORRIS, ZOO ANIMALS CELEBRATE!"

The next day, Morris and Max the Magician did the best magic show anyone had ever seen. All of the animals cheered.

At the end of the show, Morris said, "Pansy, you are the smartest and best dog in the world. Can we be best friends forever?"

"Woof, woof," I said and licked his cheek.
Avery said, "I love you, Pansy."